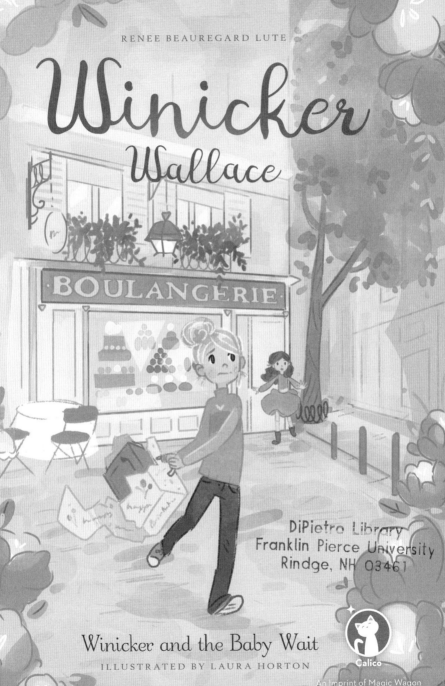

RENEE BEAUREGARD LUTE

Winicker
Wallace

BOULANGERIE

Winicker and the Baby Wait

ILLUSTRATED BY LAURA HORTON

Calico

An Imprint of Magic Wagon
abdopublishing.com

For Maddie, Simon, and Cecily, who inspire me, for Zach, who encourages me, and for my mom, who's told even her hair stylist about Winicker. –RL

To my brother Michael, who is always there to remind me that I am good enough. –LH

abdopublishing.com

Published by Magic Wagon, a division of ABDO, PO Box 398166, Minneapolis, Minnesota 55439. Copyright © 2018 by Abdo Consulting Group, Inc. International copyrights reserved in all countries. No part of this book may be reproduced in any form without written permission from the publisher. Calico™ is a trademark and logo of Magic Wagon.

Printed in the United States of America, North Mankato, Minnesota.
102017
012018

THIS BOOK CONTAINS RECYCLED MATERIALS

Written by Renee Beauregard Lute
Illustrated by Laura Horton
Edited by Heidi M.D. Elston
Art Directed by Laura Mitchell

Publisher's Cataloging-in-Publication Data

Names: Lute, Renee Beauregard, author. | Horton, Laura, illustrator.
Title: Winicker and the baby wait / by Renee Beauregard Lute; illustrated by Laura Horton.
Description: Minneapolis, Minnesota : Magic Wagon, 2018. | Series: Winicker Wallace
Summary: Winicker Wallace's mother is pregnant, and Winicker dreads the arrival of her baby brother. She can't talk to anyone about how she feels. When Winicker decides to run away from home, she finds out just how much she matters to the people she loves. Winicker's mother follows her all the way to the top of the Eiffel Tower and goes into labor in the most inconvenient place. When they finally make it to the bottom, Winicker realizes she is actually looking forward to the safe birth of her baby brother.
Identifiers: LCCN 2017946577 | ISBN 9781532130496 (lib.bdg.) | ISBN 9781532131097 (ebook) | ISBN 9781532131394 (Read-to-me ebook)
Subjects: LCSH: Mothers and daughters--Juvenile fiction. | Runaway children--Juvenile fiction. | Siblings--Juvenile fiction. | Emotions--Juvenile fiction.
Classification: DDC [FIC]--dc23
LC record available at https://lccn.loc.gov/2017946577

Things I Hate about the Baby

Dear Reader,

I don't know your actual real name, so just pretend your name is in the place where I wrote "Reader."

There are some French and Spanish words in this book, because this book takes place in Paris. When you see a French or Spanish word that you don't know, just flip to the back of the book! There is a glossary back there that will tell you what *bonjour* and *merci* mean, and lots of other French and Spanish words, too.

I know what you are thinking. "Wow, thank you so much! That is really helpful."

You're welcome. I hope you enjoy this very amazing and hilarious story.

Love,
Winicker

One

I like Paris. I like pain au chocolat. I even usually like Mirabel Plouffe, my FBFANDN (French best friend and next door neighbor). I like all kinds of things.

That's why it is very unfair of Grandma Balthazar to say, "Oh Winicker, you don't like anything." I do like things. I like millions of things. It's not my fault I don't like babies, but Grandma Balthazar is frustrated at me anyway.

It is a rainy Friday afternoon, and Grandma Balthazar is sitting across from me at the kitchen table. She looks very glamorous with her silver hair in a fancy pile on top of her head and gold buttons on her shirt. Glamorous and frustrated.

I look very unglamorous in my favorite orange nightgown with a giant cowboy boot on the front. My hair is silver too, from a certain incident where I may have used Grandma Balthazar's hair dye. It is not in a fancy pile on the top of my head. It is in a single sad bun.

When I lived in Three Rivers, Massachusetts, I always wore my hair in two buns on top of my head. When my family moved to Paris a few months ago, I protested with a single, sad bun. But when I decided to give Paris a chance, I started wearing my two buns again.

Now everything is different. Everything is awful. I am wearing a single sad bun again, because in three weeks I am getting a new baby brother. And I am protesting.

I can't think of anything worse than a baby brother. Maybe crocodiles that crawl up through the sewer and sneak into my room and bite my feet off would be worse than a baby brother. But

I don't think so. A baby brother won't bite my feet off (probably). But he will be loud. And he will be smelly.

Maizy Durand told me all about baby brothers, because she has one. I wouldn't normally trust Maizy Durand, because she's mean and awful, but that probably makes her an expert in awful things. Like baby brothers. I bet she knows a lot about sewer crocodiles, too.

She told me he'll cry all night long. And that he'll spit up all over the place. He'll make our whole apartment smell like poop. She said Mom and Dad won't do anything fun with me. I believe her because the baby isn't born yet, and Mom and Dad already don't do anything fun with me.

Mom just walks around with her hand on her back, groaning about being sore and tired. Dad gives her back rubs and builds dumb baby furniture all day long.

When Dad is building dumb baby furniture, he says words I'm not allowed to say. When I tell him: "Hey! We're not supposed to say that word!" he gets mad at me, which doesn't make any sense. When I say a bad word, I get in trouble. And when Dad says a bad word, I get in trouble!

Right this very second, Mom is napping on the couch in the living room. She's napping on a perfectly good Friday afternoon, when she could be taking me to the Eiffel Tower, where I have never been, not even once. Or the Parc Zoologique de Paris. I've been there, but I want to go again. They have penguins.

The only good thing about the baby is that Mom is always hungry, so there are always des pains au chocolat in our kitchen, bought fresh every day because Mom says old bread makes her want to vomit. Everything makes her want to vomit, but I get in trouble when I say that, too.

Grandma Balthazar cuts one pain au chocolat down the middle and passes half to me. "You know, you didn't like Paris right away, either. You complained about the rain, and you complained about all the new people and things. Remember?"

I do remember. But I don't think we need to bring up things I got in trouble for a billion weeks ago.

"Remember how Mirabel drove you crazy at first? And now you're best friends?"

I remember that too, kind of. Mirabel Plouffe is my FBFANDN. Roxanne is my best friend in Massachusetts. It's nice having best friends in two places.

"It will be like that with your baby brother. Maybe you aren't excited about him now, but when you meet him, I'm sure you will fall in love, just like you did with Paris."

"And I'm sure I won't," I say. I scoop some chocolate out of my pain au chocolat and lick it off my finger. "Do you want to watch a movie in our pajamas?"

"I'm already dressed," Grandma Balthazar says. "And anyway, I'm going to a baby boutique to buy a couple of things for your mother's baby shower."

I puff out my cheeks like a balloon.

"Do you want to come with me?" Grandma Balthazar stands up and brings her plate to the sink. She's been trying to get me to buy a gift for Mom's baby shower for weeks now, but it's not going to work. This is part of my protest.

"I'd rather get my feet bit off by sewer crocodiles." I stuff the end of the croissant into my mouth before I say something I know will get me in more trouble.

"Suit yourself," says Grandma Balthazar. She takes her coat off its hook and slides into it. "But you're going to need to shop for your own shower gift soon. The shower is in two days!"

Grandma Balthazar blows me a kiss and whirls out of the kitchen and into the rain. Her flowy gray coat swirls around her like a very glamorous tornado.

I do not want to shop for the baby shower. Dad said there will be cake, which I like, but he also said there will be baby-themed games like Guess Which Candy Bars Are Melted In These Diapers, which is just gross. I don't want to look at anything in a diaper. I also don't want to watch Mom open baby presents for hours.

Mom and Dad can force me to go to the shower. They can probably even force me to bring a gift. But they can't force me to be excited.

My gift for the baby is probably going to be a one-way ticket to Canberra, Australia. It is exactly ten thousand five hundred and seven miles away from Paris. I looked it up.

I bring my plate to the sink and hear a loud *snarghgh! snarghgh!* from the living room. Mom's snoring is terrible now that she is pregnant. She takes a lot of afternoons off so she can rest at home, but all the snoring means nobody else can rest. Or do their homework.

But I'm not going to think about the baby for the rest of the afternoon.

I take my jacket off the hook next to the stove and button it over my cowboy boot nightgown. I stick my feet into my nubby gray tabby cat slippers. Then I scribble a note on the notepad next to the kitchen door.

Family,

I am going next door to Mirabel Plouffe's, where we are not going to talk about babies or baby showers or gifts for babies.

Love,

Winicker

I shut the door behind me and run the rainy seven steps it takes to get to Mirabel Plouffe's apartment. I knock on the Plouffes' door, and Mirabel Plouffe opens it almost right away.

At least, I think it's Mirabel Plouffe at the door. I can't actually tell at first, because the

door-opener is holding a huge blue-and-white cake that looks like it's made out of diapers, blankets, tiny socks, and bottles. There's a little blue duck on top.

"Bonjour, Winicker!" my FBFANDN, Mirabel Plouffe, pokes her head out from behind the diaper cake. Her elbow is holding the door open and she seems kind of wobbly.

"Do you like it?" she asks. "I spent all afternoon working on it with my mother. It is for your mother's baby shower!"

I take a deep breath. Then I take an even deeper breath. My nubby gray tabby cat slippers are getting soaked.

"Mirabel Plouffe, you drive me crazy!" I spin around in my squishy slippers and run all seven steps back home.

I lie facedown on my puffy, blue comforter. I am soggy. My nightgown is soggy. Now my bed is soggy, too.

There won't be any more pains au chocolat until Mom wakes up and goes to the bakery to buy some. Mom is still snoring on the couch in the living room, probably dreaming mushy dreams about fat babies in blue pajamas.

Grandma Balthazar is out shopping for the baby. Even Mirabel Plouffe is making things for the baby. No one is thinking about me.

Someone knocks on my bedroom door.

"You can come in as long as you promise not to say the word *baby*," I mumble into my comforter.

Dad opens the door a crack. "I didn't catch that. Can I come in? I followed the wet footprints all the way from the kitchen to your door. So I figured you might be in here."

"Fine," I say. I sit up.

Dad opens the door the rest of the way. He looks tired. There is a thumbprint smudge on one of his eyeglass lenses, and his hair is kind of mussed up. When he looks like that, it means he's been writing. He's a writer.

"What did you write?" I ask.

"I wrote seventeen sentences, and then I deleted fourteen of them." He sits down on the edge of my bed.

"Then you only have three sentences," I say. "That's not very many."

"I miss the good ole days when you didn't know how to subtract," Dad says. He runs a hand through his hair, mussing it up even worse.

I miss those days, too. Not because I don't like subtracting. But in the good ole days we lived in Three Rivers, Massachusetts. I had my best friend Roxanne who would never, ever make a diaper cake.

In the good ole days, there was no baby brother on the way. In the good ole days, Mom didn't fall asleep on the couch and snore all weekend. In the good ole days, Grandma Balthazar only bought presents for me.

Thinking about the good ole days makes me feel kind of prickly behind my eyeballs.

"Your mom's baby shower is Sunday," Dad says.

I blink fast so tears don't come out. Everybody sounds disappointed at me when I cry because of the new baby. Disappointed is the worst sound.

"You should start thinking about what kind of present you want to give your new baby brother," he says. "Maybe you could go shopping with me or Grandma Balthazar this weekend. Or you could make something all by yourself.

"I'm sure you're feeling a little bit like you're getting lost in the shuffle, but you aren't. We love you very much, and I know your new brother is going to love you, too. You're the big sister, you know. That's a really important job. Maybe you can come up with a special gift that'll let your brother know you love him, too."

A big, cold lump forms right at the bottom of my stomach. I don't love my brother. I've never even met him! But I can't say that to Dad or Mom or Grandma Balthazar. None of them have met the baby either, but they all love him a lot. More than they love me.

How do they know he isn't going to be a really bad baby, anyway? How do they know he isn't going to turn out to be the kind of baby who throws mashed parsnip at waiters or robs banks? Or the kind of baby who yanks on his sister's hair? They don't know that! And I bet a million bucks he's going to be exactly that kind of baby.

The baby's going to be born and come live with us, and there's nothing anybody can do about that. I just wish we could go one single day without talking about it.

Two

EVERYBODY IS TOO
BUSY WITH BABY STUFF

We are all at the table on Saturday morning. Everybody is talking about the baby again. I smash my cold oatmeal around in my bowl with the back of my spoon.

Grandma Balthazar calls it "overnight oats." She keeps feeding it to all of us because it's healthy. It has weird seeds in it. I wish we could just have regular hot oatmeal without seeds again. But Grandma Balthazar says, "It's good for the baby."

If it's good for the baby, why do I have to eat it?

At least the sun is shining. When the sun shines in Paris, everybody acts as excited as if it's Christmas.

Sunny days are the exact best days to go to the Eiffel Tower. We wouldn't get all wet. And we could eat hunks of bread and cheese on the grass in front of it.

I set my glass of milk down too hard, and some milk sloshes onto the table. "Let's go to the Eiffel Tower! I've never ever been there, and it's nice out, and—"

"Winicker, please wipe up your milk. I won't be able to keep cleaning up after you once the baby comes!" Mom hands me a cloth napkin.

I hate cloth napkins. Back in Three Rivers we used paper towels. I liked using paper towels. Mom never made me bring my paper towels to the hamper. And she never got mad when I wiped up paint with paper towels. But she gets very mad when I do that with cloth napkins.

"And we can stop at your favorite bakery on the way to the Eiffel Tower and get some pains au chocolat," I say. Me and Mom both love pain

au chocolat. Especially the kind from Babette Barrett Boulangerie.

"No, Winicker. Dad and I have a lot of work to do in the nursery today."

The "nursery" is just a corner of Mom and Dad's room with a crib in it. While the baby's a baby he's going to sleep in their room. When he isn't a baby anymore, they want to stick him in my room. With me. Which will be awful.

"We'll go to the Eiffel Tower another time," Mom says.

"And anyway," Dad says, "We're going to Babette Barrett Boulangerie tomorrow for the shower. We'll get you pain au chocolat then."

"Ughhh," I groan. "I am already tired of the baby, and he isn't even here yet!"

I put my glass down too hard again, and more milk spills onto the table. I don't wipe it up this time, though. I look around the table at all three people making mad faces at me.

Nobody wants me around. All I do is spill milk and think mean thoughts.

I've got an idea for a baby shower gift after all.

It's probably the greatest gift of all time.

I'm going to get the new baby his very own room, and he won't have to share it with anyone.

One of the worst parts about living far away from my best friend Roxanne is that it is never a good time to call her on the phone.

When I lived in Three Rivers, I called Roxanne every day right after school.

Mom once said, "Why do you girls need to call each other? You were in school together all day! You should work on your homework after school instead of gabbing on the phone."

So I told her that I guess we could gab to each other all day at school instead of paying attention to Mrs. Autumn-Robert. But probably that would make Mrs. Autumn-Robert really upset, because then we wouldn't learn anything. We wouldn't be listening. We'd just be talking.

And then we could sit down and do our homework as soon as we got home, because we wouldn't be gabbing on the phone. But we wouldn't know how to do our homework because we were too busy gabbing at school to learn anything from Mrs. Autumn-Robert.

Mom did a loud sigh and let me call Roxanne after that.

When I used to call Roxanne after school, it was 2:00 in the afternoon for me, and it was 2:00 in the afternoon for Roxanne. Now that I live in Paris, our times are all messed up.

When it is 2:00 in the afternoon here, it is 8:00 in the morning in Three Rivers. Whenever I call Roxanne at 2:00 in the afternoon here, Roxanne's Granny Bee answers the phone and says, "Winicker Wallace, do you know what time it is? It's breakfast time! We're eating breakfast, honey."

Thinking about breakfast at Roxanne's house makes my mouth water.

Granny Bee makes a special kind of breakfast drink called chocolate de agua from when she used to live in the Dominican Republic. It tastes kind of cinnamony. Granny Bee serves it in Santa mugs, even if it's July.

When I used to have breakfast at Roxanne's house, we'd have bread and jelly with our chocolate de agua.

Right now it is 1:00 in the afternoon in Paris. That means it is 7:00 in the morning in Three Rivers.

Mom and Dad are out shopping for a special kind of trash can that's just for diapers. Gross. Grandma Balthazar is in the living room watching an old French movie.

I know Roxanne's family isn't having breakfast yet. Breakfast at Roxanne's house is at 8:00 in the morning.

I sit on a stool at the kitchen counter, pick up the phone, and dial Roxanne's number.

"¿Aló?" Granny Bee picks up after just one ring. "Yes?"

"Hi, Granny Bee! It's Winicker Wallace," I say. My heart does a happy little jump. It's nice to hear Granny Bee's voice.

"Winicker Wallace, it is 7:00 in the morning! It's Saturday!" Granny Bee says.

"Oh," I say. "Were you eating breakfast?" Maybe they eat breakfast earlier on Saturdays.

"No, I was sleeping! Are you all right? Is your mother all right? Is it time for el bebé already?"

"No!" I say. "No, I just wanted to talk to Roxanne. Can I? Is she awake?"

I hear rustling sounds, and then I hear my favorite voice in the whole wide world.

"Winicker!" says Roxanne.

"Roxanne!" I say. "I miss you so much!"

"I miss you, too!" says Roxanne.

We always say "I miss you" every time we talk. That's because we miss each other.

"Roxanne, take the phone into your room. I'm going back to sleep," says Granny Bee, pretty loudly. Then I hear footsteps. A door closes.

"What's up, Winicker? You're almost a sister! You gotta send me pictures of the baby when—"

"That's why I called you," I say. "The baby is ruining everything. They're going to put him in my room. They don't care that I don't want to share my room. They don't care about me anymore."

"Of course they do! Your mom and dad love you. Grandma Balthazar loves you! They're probably just excited. After the baby's been around for awhile, I bet everything will go back to normal."

"Maybe you're right," I say, but I know she is not right. "But until things get back to normal, can I come visit you and Granny Bee?"

This is the first part of my plan to get my brother his own room. I know Roxanne will say yes. This is the easy part.

"What! Winicker, you are always welcome here! Granny Bee said that right before you left Three Rivers! She said, 'that girl can visit whenever she wants.' Come visit!"

I don't tell Roxanne that I am going to move in with her forever. Once I get to her house, I'll be so helpful they'll ask me never to go back to Paris. I'll load the dishwasher and feed their golden doodle, Lincoln. I'll never wake anybody up at 7:00 in the morning again.

"Okay," I say. "I'll ask Mom and Dad when I can come!"

We say good-bye. I hang up the phone with the biggest smile I've had in weeks. This plan is working out perfectly.

Three

I can't just run away. I have to pack. I have to leave a good-bye note. I have to get a whole lot of money to pay for my taxi to the airport and my plane ticket to America.

And I have to move all of my secret stuff that I don't want Mom, Dad, and Grandma Balthazar to find out about. I start with the secret stuff.

They're going to be mad that I ran away. But when I call them from Roxanne's house in Three Rivers, they'll be so relieved to hear my voice that they will forget all about being mad and go back to talking about the baby.

But if they open up the plastic tote in my closet, they'll remember to be mad. The tote is supposed to just be full of winter stuff, like

coats and sweaters. But the coats and sweaters are on top. There are other things hidden on the bottom. Bad things.

The library book.

When I was nine years old, I still lived in Three Rivers, Massachusetts. I checked out *Beezus and Ramona* from the Palmer Public Library. Dad said, "Remember we're moving to Paris in three months, Winicker, so don't lose track of that book."

Obviously I didn't think I was going to lose track of the book. So I said I wouldn't. But then I did. The library kept calling, so I lied and told Dad I returned it even though I didn't.

Well. Then I found the book right before we moved, and I panicked. I packed it in my suitcase. I brought it to Paris. I probably owe the Palmer Public Library a billion dollars now.

The broken lipstick.

Mom runs the Paris office of a fashion website. People go to the website and buy things. Then, my mom's company mails those things to their houses.

Sometimes Mom brings home makeup and clothes to try out before she puts them on the website. One time, she brought home a lipstick that Grandma Balthazar called très chic. It was see-through and kind of blue, but it changed color if you were mad or happy.

Mom said not to touch it. But I went into her makeup box, and I did touch it. And the lipstick part broke off the holder part. I flushed the lipstick part down the toilet and hid the holder part in my tote.

Mom figured she misplaced the lipstick, and I never told her she didn't.

The bra.

When we moved to Paris, Grandma Balthazar got a lot fancier. Her hair got fancier, her clothes got fancier, and her bras got fancier.

She bought one bra that had red jewels shaped like raindrops on it. I took the bra so I could try to paint a picture of it for Roxanne.

But when I was painting it, I spilled the paint. I got it all over me and the letter and the bra. And one of Mom's cloth napkins. Grandma Balthazar asked me if I knew where the bra went, but I just made gagging sounds like bras are gross. She never asked me about it again.

I can't just put these things in the trash, because Mom looks in the trash. That's how she found out about the napkin. I won't make that mistake again.

I stuff the secret things into my green backpack, and then I pack some things on top of them. Two shirts. A pair of jeans. A couple of granola bars. My favorite book in the whole world, *The Mouse and the Motorcycle*. My passport. Then I sit down at my desk and write.

Family,

I am moving back to Three Rivers. I hope you don't feel too bad about having a new baby that you love more than me and not taking me to the Eiffel Tower. I'll be fine. Please mail me my stuff when you get a few minutes.

Love,

The only thing I have left to do is get a bunch of money to travel. Grandma Balthazar told me once that a plane ticket from Paris to Boston is nine hundred euros. That's about a thousand dollars in American money.

I know it's that much because Dad and I saw a fancy diaper bag in a store window in the Latin Quarter a couple of weeks ago. We went inside so he could ask how much the bag was. The man in the store said, "nine hundred euros," and Dad said, "nine hundred euros! That's a thousand dollars in American money! A thousand dollars for a diaper bag? A thousand dollars!"

Dad didn't buy the diaper bag.

I can't ask Mom or Dad or Grandma Balthazar for nine hundred euros. They will want to know why I need all that money. They won't give me that much if I say it's for that diaper bag. I sit down on my bed and think.

Who can help me? Who likes to help everyone? Who is the most annoyingly helpful person in the whole entire world?

I am going to ask Mirabel Plouffe.

Not only is Mirabel Plouffe annoying, but she has the whitest living room in the world. The couch is white. The chairs are white. The rug and walls and shelves are white. Even though I'm not dirty, I'm scared I'm going to get everything dirty. I will definitely never paint in here.

"I'm sorry I said you drive me crazy yesterday," I say. I brush invisible dirt off my pants. "I am having a hard time with the fact that my mom is having a baby and not taking me to the Eiffel Tower. That's why I came over."

When a kid says "I'm having a hard time," grown-ups are a little nicer to them. But when I say the word *baby*, I see Mirabel Plouffe's eyeballs go all watery and happy. She isn't listening about my hard time. She is just listening about the baby.

"Oh, the baby! I cannot wait until the baby is here," she says.

"Yes, well," I say, "about the baby. I'm just in the way at home, now, so I think it's time for me to—"

"To buy the baby a present!" Mirabel Plouffe flutters her hands around like they're a couple of birds. "Oui! I knew you would give up your protest! Your mother's shower is tomorrow, so there is not very much time!"

There is no way Mirabel Plouffe is going to give me money to fly back to America. She doesn't know how bad it feels to not be the only one anymore. She's not the one getting stuck with a poopy baby brother. She's not the one whose family doesn't even pay attention to her anymore.

But wait! My brain goes lightbulb-y, like in a cartoon when somebody gets a good idea. Mirabel Plouffe won't give me money to run away, but I bet she'll give me money for a baby shower present!

"Yes!" I say. "There's not much time. But the problem is, the present I really want to give the baby is expensive. And I don't have any money."

Mirabel Plouffe's face gets a little concerned looking, but also very excited looking, because she loves to help. Helping is Mirabel Plouffe's favorite thing, next to old bookstores and the afternoon news. Mirabel Plouffe is weird.

"Quel dommage. But maybe I can help you! I can give you a little money for a baby shower gift!"

"Really?" I try to act surprised, like I didn't think of it myself. "Thanks, Mirabel Plouffe! I need nine hundred euros. That should cover the cost of the present and wrapping paper." Mirabel Plouffe's eyes get really big. I scratch my knee. "And . . . a bow. A really nice bow."

"Nine hundred euros? Winicker!" She laughs louder than I've ever heard her laugh before. "I have ten euros!"

She tries to catch her breath from laughing so hard. "Nine hundred! Ho!" She starts laughing again, and I get an itchy, annoyed feeling.

"Okay, thanks. But I have to go find some money, so . . ."

"I will go get the ten euros. You are welcome to it. And maybe you will get lucky! Maybe you will find the next bag of money from Monsieur Generous."

"Huh?" I never know what Mirabel Plouffe is talking about.

"Monsieur Generous! He has been on the afternoon news! He has been leaving bags of one thousand euros at different landmarks in Paris. Last week, an old woman found one of the bags at the Louvre. On Thursday, a man found another bag at the Arc de Triomphe. Maybe you will find the next bag!"

One thousand euros! My brain goes lightbulb-y again.

The Eiffel Tower.

There's got to be a bag from Monsieur Generous at the Eiffel Tower! I can't get anybody in my family to take me there. But Mom's baby shower will be right down the street from the Eiffel Tower. And the shower is tomorrow!

One thousand euros is enough for the taxi to the airport and the plane ride and the bus to Roxanne's house in Three Rivers. Now I just have to figure out how I'm going to get my suitcase to the baby shower without making everybody suspicious.

Four

I HAVE TO GO TO THE BABY SHOWER

On Sunday morning, everyone is dressed up for the baby shower. Grandma Balthazar's gifts for Mom and the baby are wrapped in blue paper on the coffee table in the living room. I set my suitcase down next to them with a *thunk*.

Mom smiles at Dad like I'm the greatest kid ever. Grandma Balthazar smiles at me like I'm the greatest kid ever. I don't smile at anybody, because I don't feel like the greatest kid ever.

I wrapped my suitcase in wrapping paper that says Happy Birthday all over it. That's all the wrapping paper I could find in our craft closet. That's how I'm going to get the suitcase to the baby shower. It's in disguise.

"I can't wait to see your gift, Winicker," says Mom. I shrug like it's no big deal. My stomach feels a little flip-floppy, like maybe running away to America isn't the best idea in the world.

"I'm so proud of—oh! A big kick! This little guy knows it's his party today. Want to feel?" Mom rubs her belly. Grandma Balthazar and Dad jump up from the couch to ooh and ahh all over the baby who isn't even here yet.

"Hey, do you think we could go to the Eiffel Tower after—"

"No, Winicker!" Dad looks up from Mom's belly. "We'll go another day. Today you and Mom and Grandma Balthazar are going to be really busy. And anyway, the Eiffel Tower is a pretty long walk from the bakery. Please don't tire your mom out!"

On second thought, maybe running away to America is the best idea in the world.

Babette Barrett Boulangerie is the best bakery in Paris. It always smells like chocolate. Whenever we come, Mom and Grandma Balthazar order a coffee, and Madame Barrett brings me foamy warm milk in a fancy mug.

I wish it were just Mom and Grandma Balthazar and me now. I wish there weren't a banner that says Bienvenue, Baby Boy Wallace in gold letters on the wall.

It's a small bakery, so Mom's baby shower makes everything feel squeezy and too close.

We are sitting in a circle around three café tables. There's me, Mom, Grandma Balthazar, Mirabel Plouffe, Mirabel Plouffe's mom, and three French women Mom works with.

The women are Anne, Laure, and Lenae. When Mom talks about them at home, she just calls them The Ladies.

The Ladies all have the same chopped haircuts and pointy witch shoes. I guess pointy witch shoes are going to be stylish soon. The Ladies always wear what's going to be stylish soon.

I hope witch hats are also going to be stylish soon. I have a witch hat in my closet. But then my stomach gets kind of heavy feeling when I remember I won't be here in Paris to wear my witch hat. I will be in Three Rivers. Maybe I should have packed it.

"Ma choupette," says one of the pointy shoe women. She's looking at me. "Look at that silver hair. Big sister, what is your name again? Vinegar? Vinegar, with the silver hair?"

"Winicker." My face gets hot. I look at Mirabel Plouffe for support, because she stands up for me at school when awful Maizy Durand makes my face get hot. But Mirabel Plouffe is laughing into her napkin.

Everyone is laughing.

"Vinegar?" Mom laughs so hard she drops her napkin on the floor. "Oh, goodness. Did you think my daughter's name was Vinegar all this time?"

Everyone laughs even harder. Mrs. Plouffe is laughing, and I've never seen her laugh

before. Grandma Balthazar is laughing so hard she's shaking. She wipes her eyes with her napkin.

My face is probably the temperature of the sun. I feel like crying. I feel like running away. Then I remember the plan.

I take a couple of deep breaths. I sit up very straight in my chair. I try to ignore the delicious smell of chocolate. (We haven't had cake yet. I was going to wait until after the cake, but then Vinegar happened.)

"I have to go to the bathroom," I say. No one notices. They're all still laughing.

I get up from my chair and feel for my gift-wrapped suitcase behind me. I turn around and hug the suitcase to my chest. My heart is beating very fast.

I walk toward the bathroom, but instead of going inside, I turn left. I open the door to the outside. And I run as fast as I can down the sidewalk. I run toward the Eiffel Tower.

Five

I turn the corner and run down another street. A loooooong street. The longest street I've ever run down. Finally, I reach the Champ de Mars, a great big park in front of the Eiffel Tower.

I know a lot about the Eiffel Tower. I have a guidebook all about it. I told Mom and Dad and Grandma Balthazar lots of facts from my book all the time because I wanted to go. But they just wanted to talk about baby stuff.

One time I said, "Did you know the Eiffel Tower is always taller in the summer? Heat makes the metal expand by up to six inches!"

Grandma Balthazar said, "Oh, Alice, look at the baby swing in this catalog. It has five speeds!"

I stop running. I can hardly breathe! I set the suitcase down on the sidewalk and rest my hands on my knees for a minute. Whew.

The Eiffel Tower always seemed closer when I drank my foamy milk at Babette Barrett Boulangerie. Dad was right. It's a pretty long walk. Ladies wearing big hats and men with fancy shoes are walking little dogs on leashes.

I'm still catching my breath when a hand lands on my shoulder.

"Aaaaah!" I yell. I whirl around. It's Mirabel Plouffe! She's catching her breath too.

"Winicker! What—" She holds up one finger and breathes hard for a few seconds. "What are you doing? Why did you run from your mother's baby shower?"

"Because I'm going home, Mirabel Plouffe!"

"Home?" Mirabel Plouffe crinkles up her forehead. "All by yourself? Are you looking for the Métro—"

"No!" I lift up my suitcase and tear the wrapping paper off a corner. "It's my suitcase. I'm going to my real home! I'm going to Three Rivers. Where I won't get stuck with a baby and parents who don't care about me anymore."

Mirabel Plouffe stumbles backward a little like she got pushed. "Winicker Wallace! You cannot go back to America alone! You cannot go back to America at all! Your parents will be so sad. I will be so sad!"

I feel a little bad. Mirabel Plouffe does look kind of so sad.

"I have to go. There isn't space for me anymore in my apartment. There isn't even space for me in my own family." When I say the word *family* my face gets hot, and my throat gets tickly.

"Oh, Winicker." Mirabel Plouffe looks like she is going to cry.

I know what she is going to say. She's going to say let's go back to your mother's baby shower.

She's going to say running away isn't the answer. She's probably right. I should probably listen.

"If you must run away to America, let me help you. How are you planning to get to the airport? How are you going to pay for your flight? Why did you run this way, to La Tour Eiffel?"

Mirabel Plouffe is a very surprising person, sometimes.

"I'm at the Eiffel Tower because of Monsieur Generous. There's got to be a bag of money here! You said he's leaving them at all of the landmarks in Paris. The Eiffel Tower is the most famous landmark here!"

Mirabel Plouffe nods her head wisely. "You may be right. We will try to find it."

I pick up my suitcase, and we both walk toward the Eiffel Tower. We walk through the long park, and then we walk through a big crowd of people who are taking pictures of the Eiffel Tower.

We stop walking again. Both of us look up. It's so tall. It's 984 feet, according to my guidebook. And, 984 feet and 6 inches in the summer. I almost fall over backward trying to see the top of it! It looks just like all the magazine pictures of the Eiffel Tower Mom stuck to the fridge at our house in Three Rivers when she told us we were going to move here.

My heart feels kind of good achy because I'm going back home to Three Rivers. But it also feels kind of bad achy because I'm leaving my family and my home in Paris. And Mirabel Plouffe, who always turns out to be a good friend right when I think she's going to be the most annoying.

It's not so great to have home be in two places, because then you feel homesick no matter where you are.

We reach the maze of a million people in line to buy tickets.

"Why is this line so long?" I ask.

"Because this is La Tour Eiffel," Mirabel Plouffe says. "Everyone wants to see it! But Winicker, your suitcase! You cannot bring it with you! Not in line, and not to La Tour Eiffel."

I look down at my suitcase that is still mostly wrapped in Happy Birthday paper. Then I look up at all of the security guards wearing small black hats and very serious faces. They are everywhere.

One of the security guards points at a lady's purse. He shakes his head no. The lady steps out of line and looks very disappointed. A man with a small backpack leaves the line, too.

Mirabel Plouffe reaches for my suitcase. "I will wait for you down here. I will stay with your suitcase. You go, Winicker. You find your treasure."

She really is a very good friend.

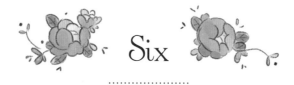

Six

POOPY DIAPERS

I get in line by myself. I wait and wait. I move forward a step or two every couple of minutes. I always thought running away would be more exciting than this. Or at least faster. After a very, very long time, I get to the ticket booth.

"Bonjour!" The woman selling tickets smiles at me.

"Can I have one ticket to the top, please?" I ask.

"Oui. For you, that will be eight euros."

I pay the ticket booth lady with the euros Mirabel Plouffe gave me yesterday, and I get in line for the first elevator.

It takes two elevators to get to the top of the Eiffel Tower. The first one makes my stomach feel kind of upside-down. I am packed inside and can't see anything other than grown-up backs and shoulders.

The grown-ups are all looking out the glass sides of the elevator. I bet they're seeing all kinds of neat things.

If Dad were here, he'd put me up on his shoulders so I could see, too. If Mom were here, she'd say, "excuse me," and people would move aside so I could see. People always listen to Mom, even when she's not pregnant. If Grandma Balthazar were here, she'd say, "excusez-moi," which is how French people say "excuse me."

When the elevator gets to the second floor, the doors make a very loud *buzzzzzzz*, and everyone gets out.

Some of the people from my elevator go to the restaurants on the second floor. My stomach

gurgles because I never did get any chocolate cake at Mom's baby shower, but I don't go to the restaurants.

For one thing, I don't think Monsieur Generous would leave a bag of money on the second floor of the Eiffel Tower in some old restaurant. For another, I spent almost all the money I had on my ticket.

I get on the second elevator, and I still can't see anything. More people are crowded around the sides, looking out at Paris. They're all taller than me. My stomach gets the upside-down feeling again. But this time it also gets an excited feeling, because I'm almost at the top!

I'm going to see the whole entire city. Then I'm going to find the bag of money that is going to take me back to Three Rivers and Roxanne and no babies.

When everyone piles out after the elevator *buzzzzzzzes*, I can finally see everything through the elevator walls. And I mean everything! I am so high up!

I jump out of the elevator before the door closes. I race to one of the windows in the round room the elevator took me to. I'm at the top of the Eiffel Tower! Except there is a flight of stairs a few feet away with a line of people waiting to go up. Another line. That must be the top of the Eiffel Tower. And that's where Monsieur Generous must have left a bag of money.

Finally, it is my turn to go up. The very, very top of the Eiffel Tower is all caged in, and I'm glad. I'm so high up that I can see birds flying below me. I'm so high up that I feel a little dizzy. The wind is blowing so hard I feel like I might get blown away.

I look at the floor and put my hands over my ears to block out some of the wind sound while I search.

Monsieur Generous. The bag of money. Where is the bag of money?

There are just ten other people on the top floor with me. None of them look like they're looking for a bag of money.

I walk all around the caged edges of the top. I don't see anything that looks like a bag of money.

What if I'm wrong? What if Monsieur Generous didn't leave a bag of money on top of the Eiffel Tower after all? Or what if he did, but someone else found it already?

I keep looking. I walk around a second time. And then a third time. Maybe it would be in a bag with a dollar sign on it, like in a movie? Probably not. We're in France. It would have a euro sign on it. Or maybe it would look like a purse? Or a lunch bag?

No! It's none of those.

There is a trash bin next to a small champagne bar. Right behind the trash bin, I see it. It's a blue plastic bag.

I hurry over and crouch down next to it. The top of the bag is tied in a knot. It almost looks like trash! Monsieur Generous must be very clever.

I unknot the top of the bag with my fingers. I open it up, and . . . it smells awful. Terrible. It smells like a garbage dump on a very hot day. It smells like a pay toilet. I look inside. It smells like . . . poop.

There is a poopy diaper in the blue bag.

I feel sick to my stomach from the smell. I feel sick to my heart because there is no bag of money on top of the Eiffel Tower. There is only a bag of poop.

I climb back down the stairs and take the elevator to the second floor. People with cameras are crowded together around the edge of the Eiffel Tower. They are taking pictures of Paris and each other and themselves. They all look happy.

I sit down on the floor next to the elevator, trying not to cry. I felt pretty brave when I ran out of Babette Barrett Boulangerie. And I felt brave when I left Mirabel Plouffe at the end of the ticket line. I felt especially brave when I rode the elevator up to the top of the Eiffel Tower. But I don't feel brave now.

I was wrong about Monsieur Generous. And now I don't have any money for a plane ticket to America. And I'm going to be in really, really big trouble for running away.

I stand up and dust off my pants. I wonder if I can see Mirabel Plouffe from up here. I smoosh into the crowd so I can look down over the city.

I can see the Champ de Mars. I can see the long line of people waiting to come up. They are so tiny, they look like fleas. I can even see the end of the line where I left Mirabel Plouffe and my suitcase.

But I can't see Mirabel Plouffe. I can't see my suitcase, either. I wonder if she could hear me if I yell down to her. I stick my face against the fence.

"Mirabel Plouffe?" I yell. The lady next to me gives me a weird look. She shoos her kids over to another viewing area. "Mirabel Plouffe?" I yell a little louder. "MIRABEL PLOUFFE! MIRABEL—"

"Winicker Wallace, I am right here." I whip around, and Mirabel Plouffe is standing right behind me! My suitcase isn't next to her. But my mom is. She looks worried. But her face changes, and now she looks mad. Really, really mad. I don't think she's ever looked this mad before.

"WINICKER. WALLACE." Her voice is loud, but the wind is loud, too. She crouches down low and puts her face close to my face so I can hear her better.

"I cannot believe you would do something like this," she says. "Mirabel told me everything. Everything. You were running away to Three Rivers? What were you thinking?"

Usually when I am in trouble, I feel guilty and sad. But this time I feel mad. I feel just as mad as my mom. Maybe madder.

"I was thinking that since you don't care about me anymore, I would go live with a family that does care about me!"

I look at Mirabel Plouffe, who is looking down at her shoes. "And I was thinking that I could trust Mirabel Plouffe not to—"

"Don't you blame Mirabel Plouffe for this! She is a good friend to you. I came after you. I found Mirabel standing near the line, and I told her she needed to tell me what was going on."

"Je suis désolée. I am sorry, Winicker." Mirabel Plouffe really does look sorry.

"Don't be sorry, honey," Mom says to Mirabel Plouffe. "You did the right thing."

Then she looks at me. "You did not do the right thing." Mom's eyes are watery. "I'm so sad that you feel like we don't care about you, Winicker. Of course we care about you. We love spending time with you! But we are also trying to get ready for the baby. It's been a very busy time for us. But we've never, ever stopped caring about you! We never will!"

Her voice gets a little nicer sounding. "I wish you'd said something, Winicker. Maybe I should have been paying closer attention." She pulls me in for a hug. Her big belly is kind of in the way, but I don't mind right now. I close my eyes. I'm glad Mom came to find me.

I still wish there had been money in that bag instead of poop, though.

"Okay." Mom stands up slowly. "I'm not feeling great. Pregnant women should not run all over Paris. I need a nap. Let's take the lift down and get ourselves back to Babette Barrett Boulangerie. Mirabel, your mother is very anxious to know that you're safe. Grandma Balthazar is worried about you, too, Winicker. She stayed at the bakery in case you went back there."

"How did you know I was here, anyway?" I ask.

"It was a lucky guess," Mom says. "I do listen to you. I knew you wanted to see the Eiffel Tower."

"And here we are," says Mirabel Plouffe. "La Tour Eiffel." She makes a sweeping motion with her arm toward the guardrails.

The three of us look out over the whole big city. It looks like a gray and green pie all cut into slices. I can see for miles and miles.

"I bet we can see England from here," I say.

"We can't," says Mirabel Plouffe.

"Oh. Well, it's still cool, isn't it?" I rub my nose. It's cold from the wind.

"C'est magnifique," Mirabel Plouffe says.

"It's very cool." Mom squeezes my shoulders. "Let's go. We'll come back soon. I promise."

I don't think that's true. I don't think Mom is going to have time to come back with me soon. But I don't say that out loud. I don't want to make Mom mad and sad all over again.

Mom and Mirabel Plouffe and I pile into the glass elevator with everyone else who is ready to go back down to the bottom.

I feel a little scrunched, but then I look up at Mom, and she looks a lot scrunched. There is barely room for her and her belly on the elevator. She is making a face like—like she doesn't feel good.

"Are you okay?" I ask. The elevator starts moving.

"Not exactly," Mom says. She sits down very slowly. The people around us look nervous. "I think I'm in early labor. I think I'm going to have the baby today."

The elevator makes a loud *buzzzzzz* sound again, and it stops. But we aren't on the ground level. We're in between levels. Someone pushes the button over and over again but the elevator does not move. We are stuck!

Seven

"Madame, Madame!" Some of the strangers on the elevator rush to help my mom. Others press themselves against the sides of the elevator to give her more room. I kneel down next to her.

"Mom! What should I do? How can I help? Shouldn't you call Dad?" I hate how scared my mom looks. I've never seen her look scared before. She isn't scared of anything.

Well, that's not true. She's scared of caterpillars. But she isn't scared of anything else.

What is going to happen if the elevator takes too long to get moving again?

"I was on my phone all morning because of the baby shower." Mom rummages around in her purse until she finds her phone. She holds it up to show me and presses the button a couple of times. Nothing happens.

"I ran the battery down to nothing. I didn't realize until I found Mirabel near the line. I tried to text Mrs. Plouffe and Grandma Balthazar to let them know you were both safe, but my phone wouldn't turn on."

"J'ai besoin d'un médecin!" Mirabel Plouffe looks very white. I don't know what she's saying, but médecin sounds like medicine.

"My mom is having a baby," I say to everyone around us. "She's having a baby right now!"

Everyone starts buzzing like bees in a big glass hive. A couple of people pull out their phones and mumble the word *ambulance* into them. I hope someone is also calling for an elevator repair person.

"No, I am not," she says loudly. "Please cancel the ambulances!" Then her voice gets quieter.

"Winicker, honey. I am not having the baby right now. I have hours. Probably lots of hours. I'm just very uncomfortable, that's all." Mom is making a face like she has a bad stomachache.

I've seen enough movies to know babies are sometimes born fast. Sometimes they are born in surprising places. In fact, in the bad TV movies Grandma Balthazar used to watch in Three Rivers, most babies are born in elevators.

The people around us are making nervous sounds. They must have seen the movies, too. Someone is knocking on the glass side of the elevator as though that's going to make it start moving again.

A man wearing sunglasses and white tennis shoes puts a hand over his forehead like he's going to faint. His voice sounds American, like mine. "Oh man. Oh no. Okay, I'm going to pass out. I hate being stuck in a small space. I'm going to faint, and there isn't any room for me to faint.

Oh no." He tries to lean against the corner of the elevator.

The woman standing next to him makes a face like my mom makes when I complain about things. "Grayson, you aren't the one having a baby on the elevator of the Eiffel Tower." She crosses her arms.

The whole thing seems even worse after the woman says it out loud. My mom is going to have a baby on the elevator! She can't! She's supposed to have him in a hospital with white sheets and doctors with clean hands!

This is all my fault. If I hadn't run away, Mom wouldn't be here. She probably wouldn't even be in labor.

I hold Mom's hand because I don't know what else to do. She squeezes it gently.

"I'm sorry, Mom. I'm so, so sorry." I used to not want a baby brother. Now all I want is for him to get here safely. And for my mom to have him somewhere that's not inside an elevator.

I take a deep breath. I look at all the people squished on the elevator with us. There is a woman with a long, white scarf draped around her neck. It looks pretty soft.

"I guess we should ask that lady for her scarf," I say. "We can wrap the baby in it. Just in case."

"What? No!" Mom looks like her stomach still hurts. She also looks embarrassed. "Honey, I am not going to have the baby on this elevator. I'm sure—"

Buzzzzzzz! The elevator jolts, and we're moving again! Everyone around us makes a loud sigh of relief.

Mirabel Plouffe looks like she's seen a monster. Her face is very white, and her hands look kind of shaky.

When we reach the bottom, the doors buzz open, and all of the people near us pour out. The woman with Grayson looks back at me and Mom and Mirabel Plouffe.

"Ma'am," she says to Mom. "Can I help? Do you need something to eat? I bought a baguette and some cheese on the second floor. Please take it." She holds out a paper bag with bread sticking out the top.

"Thank you so much!" Mom says. "Actually, I'm really hungry." I feel a knot of guilt in my stomach. I'm the whole reason Mom didn't get to eat at her baby shower. I also feel hungry in my stomach. I think about the chocolate cake I didn't get to eat.

Mom takes the paper bag.

"Good luck," says the woman. She walks away, and Grayson leans on her like he's dizzy. His face is pale, like Mirabel Plouffe's.

Mirabel Plouffe is taking big deep breaths through her nose and letting them out through her mouth.

"Mirabel, honey, are you okay?" Mom offers Mirabel Plouffe a hunk of bread. Mirabel shakes her head.

"Oui, I am fine. But your phone does not work, and you are having a baby. And my mother does not know where I am!" Mirabel Plouffe sits down and pulls her knees up to her head. She goes back to doing her weird breathing again.

"Can we borrow a phone and call Mrs. Plouffe?" I ask.

"My mother doesn't believe in cell phones. She says they take us away from the world around us. She says, 'Carry a book and never a phone, and the world will be at your fingertips.'"

Mom looks a little annoyed at Mrs. Plouffe's opinion about phones. Then she just looks tired.

"I'm so sorry about all of this, Mirabel." My mom sits down next to Mirabel Plouffe, so I sit down, too. "If you're feeling brave, I have a job for you."

Mirabel Plouffe perks right up. There's nothing that makes her happier than having a job to do.

"Anything, Madame Wallace. I am feeling brave. What can I do?"

Eight

"Mirabel, you know how to get back to Babette Barrett Boulangerie, don't you?" Mom asks.

Mirabel nods. "Oui. There is only one turn. And I am a very fast runner."

"Can you run back and tell Grandma Balthazar that we're here at the Eiffel Tower? Please let her know I'm going to have the baby. Have her call Winicker's dad, too. He'll take a cab to the bakery and pick up Grandma Balthazar. Then they'll pick us up on the way to the hospital." Mom closes her eyes and frowns again.

I hope Mirabel Plouffe runs faster than she's ever run in her whole life.

"Au revoir et bonne chance," says Mirabel Plouffe. "Bon courage!" She gets down into a

runner's position, with both hands and one knee on the ground. All of a sudden, she's up and sprinting down the Champ de Mars as fast as a cheetah.

Some people stop and look at her. A couple of security guards in black hats nod at her. Everyone is impressed with Mirabel Plouffe. This time, that doesn't even make me feel annoyed. I'm impressed with her, too.

"Well, I guess it's just you and me, kiddo."
Mom's face looks worried and tired, but it also
looks kind of smiley. I wish I had never run away.

"I'm sorry, Mom." I really am sorry. I've never
felt so sorry in my whole entire life.

"I know, Winicker. Please know how much
I love you. And how much your dad and
Grandma Balthazar love you. It breaks my
heart that you thought we didn't care about you

anymore. We've been so excited to give you a baby brother!"

I hug my mom really tight. "I love you too," I say. "And Dad and Grandma Balthazar. And I'll probably even love the baby when he comes out."

Mom looks really happy that I said that. She looks so happy that she'll probably never feel sad or mad again.

She passes me a hunk of bread and a piece of cheese, and I stuff them both into my mouth. I'm having a bread and cheese picnic at the bottom of the Eiffel Tower with my mom. This day started out okay, and then got really bad. Now it's great. I hope it stays like this forever.

Except all of a sudden, there's a security guard walking toward us, and he has my suitcase. My suitcase! I forgot about that.

"Excusez-moi," he says. "I have your suitcase, Madame." He's looking at Mom. "You left it at the ticket booth." He lays the suitcase down.

"Great! Are there snacks in here?" She shows me the empty bag that used to have bread and cheese in it. "We're out, and we may be sitting here for awhile."

Before I can say anything like *Wait!* or *No!* or *Don't open that!*, Mom unzips the suitcase and opens it up. My stomach gets kind of a sink-y feeling. She looks pretty happy about the granola bars inside. But then she looks confused. She picks up the library book and looks at the library sticker on the spine.

"Is this—did you keep a library book from the Palmer Public Library?"

I squint my eyes at her like I'm not sure I know what she's talking about.

"Winicker Wallace." Now Mom doesn't look confused at all. She looks just a little bit mad. "You probably owe the Palmer Public Library a billion dollars." She sighs and puts the book back inside my suitcase. Then her face gets a lot mad.

"What in the world?" She picks up the lipstick holder. "Is this the lipstick from my office? The one you were never supposed to touch? The one that mysteriously went missing a couple of months ago?" She looks at it closer. "And where is the actual lipstick part?"

I try to think of a really good lie, but it's too late for lies. And I'm too tired for lies. And if it weren't for lies, Mom would still be smiling at me under the Eiffel Tower. "I flushed it down the toilet," I say. It actually makes me feel better to say it out loud.

"You flushed it down the toilet," Mom says. She sighs and puts the lipstick holder back. Then she holds up Grandma Balthazar's red jewel bra with the paint all over it. She shakes her head.

"I don't really know what to say about that," I say. "It's pretty much what it looks like. My paint spilled." I shrug my shoulders.

"I see." Mom lays the bra back down on top of the other stuff in the suitcase. She makes another pain face, with her eyes squeezed shut.

"Sorry about everything," I say when her face goes back to normal. "I was planning to get rid of that stuff at Roxanne's house. Then you'd never have to know about it."

"But don't you feel better now that I know?"

And actually, I do feel a little better. I feel like I just took off a super itchy sweater that I've been wearing for a long time.

"I see you packed *The Mouse and the Motorcycle*, too," she says. She picks up my book and turns it over to read the back.

"Yeah, it's still my favorite," I say. "When I was new in Paris, I felt like Ralph S. Mouse. He was pretty small in a big, scary place, like I was. And he had some bad days, too. Just like me."

Mom squeezes my shoulders. "I wonder if the baby will feel like that, too," she says.

I bet he probably will feel like that. He's going to be even smaller than I am. Mom looks like she hurts again. She closes her eyes and lets out a slow breath.

When Grandma Balthazar and Dad get here, we'll go to the hospital. And then the baby will be here. I'll tell him I'm happy he's here, because I actually do feel kind of happy about it now.

Except I wasn't happy about it before, so I didn't get him a present. I don't have anything to give him. And I ruined the baby shower. He's not even here yet, and I ruined everything.

Nine

The good news is Dad and Grandma Balthazar aren't as mad as I thought they would be.

I sat between Mom and Dad on the cab ride to the American Hospital of Paris. They both hugged me a lot. Mom kept looking at Dad over the top of my head and whispering, "She thought we didn't care about her anymore, Michael. She thought we didn't care about her anymore!" Then they'd both hug me again. I guess I was wrong about them not caring about me.

Grandma Balthazar sat in the front seat next to the driver. At first she was worried about Mom and the baby and whether we were going to get to the hospital on time.

But then she was embarrassed, and that got her mind off of being worried. She was embarrassed because I told her I was sorry for taking her red jewel bra without asking. And that I was extra sorry for spilling paint all over it and lying.

She did a really loud laugh and said, "Winicker, dear, you say the strangest things!" She looked at her lap the whole rest of the ride to the hospital.

The other good news is that we did get to the hospital on time. Only now we've been here for a lot of hours, and I keep asking Mom to hurry up, because I'm pretty tired after today.

It was a really long day.

The last time I said I was tired and bored, Mom's face got kind of red and she asked if I would like to go home. I do want to go home, but I also want to be here when my baby brother is born. Also, I don't think she was serious about letting me go home.

I'm sitting in one of the chairs by the delivery room window. Grandma Balthazar and Dad are pacing around the little white room.

Dad keeps fluffing Mom's pillow, even though she asked him to stop fluffing it about four fluffs ago.

Grandma Balthazar is taking pictures of everything in the room with her phone. A picture of me. A picture of the pile of baby shower gifts on the chair next to me. A picture of Mom trying to sleep. A picture of Dad fluffing Mom's pillow for the thirtieth time.

The baby shower gifts remind me of how sad I am about not having anything to give the baby.

But then I get a jumpy, excited feeling in my stomach. It feels like I have an amazing idea. It feels like I have the best idea on earth.

"Mom," I say, "Can I give the baby a name?"

Mom opens one of her eyes. "You want to name the baby?"

"Yes! I already have a million good ideas. Eiffel Tower Wallace. Baby Balthazar Wallace. Winicker Wallace Jr."

Dad looks at Mom. They look at each other. Then they look at me.

"Honey," Dad says, "we already have a name picked out."

"Oh," I say. I look at my shoes. "Never mind."

I hate when I have the best idea on earth and nobody else thinks so. I also hate that I'm starting my job as a big sister by being a really awful big sister who runs away and doesn't have a present for her baby brother.

I look at the pile of gifts. There's a big square one that probably has something not very fun in it, like some kind of baby equipment. Big square presents always look exciting and fun, but then they turn out to be a vibrating toothbrush kit.

There are two rectangle presents on top of the square one. I bet there are baby clothes inside.

Then there are five smaller, flatter boxes on top of the rectangle ones. Those look like books. Probably board books. Probably about animals like baby ducks and bears and mice.

I get an even better idea than my other idea. I get the best idea in the whole world. I know what I'm going to give my new baby brother.

Mom gasps really loudly, and everybody looks at her.

"Get the doctor, please. I'm going to have the baby."

Ten

I'LL BE STUCK WITH THE BABY
IN OUR FAMILY FOREVER

I'm a big sister! I didn't think I liked babies. In all the movies I've seen and all the stories I've heard—especially from mean, awful Maizy Durand—babies aren't very interesting. They cry and spit up a lot and then spend the rest of their time sleeping.

But not my new baby brother! His name is Walter Wallace, and he has a whole head of brown hair. It's kind of parted on one side, like he works in a bank.

I got to hold him at the hospital right after he was born. At first he was red and kind of wet and I didn't want to hold him.

But Dad put him in my arms anyway, and Walter looked frowny like he wasn't so sure he

liked being born. I smiled at him so he wouldn't be sad, and he raised one of his little eyebrows at me. It wasn't so bad holding him. And it's not so bad having a baby brother.

He doesn't cry very much. He doesn't spit up very much, either. He sleeps a lot, but when he's awake he is the best baby in the whole world. He listens to me when I talk. He has a very serious face. And he likes when I read to him from *The Mouse and the Motorcycle*, which is my very favorite book in the world.

That's the present I gave him the day he was born: my *The Mouse and the Motorcycle* paperback. Mom and Dad and Grandma Balthazar said, "Are you sure? That's your favorite book!"

I'm sure. Walter is very small in a very big world. Just like Ralph S. Mouse. I even wrote Walter a note inside the book cover.

Dear Walter,

This will be your favorite book.

Love,

Winicker

It is Saturday morning. Mom and Walter have been home from the hospital for five days. I'm eating cinnamon toast at the kitchen table. Walter is watching me from his bouncer.

"This is toast," I tell him. "It isn't great, but it's what we have for breakfast sometimes. It's better than cold oatmeal."

"Winicker," Mom says. "Please finish your toast and get dressed. The Ladies from the office are coming by this morning to meet Walter."

The Ladies. The awful ones with the pointy shoes. The ones who called me Vinegar. I do a kind of shiver, because that was a really bad day.

But then it was a really good day, because it was the day Walter was born.

I look over at Walter again, and he is looking at me. I stuff the rest of my toast in my mouth and point to my face so Mom knows I'm finished eating.

When I'm all dressed, Dad asks me to help dress Walter while he helps Mom and Grandma Balthazar pick up the kitchen and living room.

The kitchen and living room need more picking up than usual these days.

Ever since Walter was born, there are dishes on the kitchen counter and crumbs under the table and burp cloths all over the place.

Yesterday, Grandma Balthazar found a tiny wet diaper all rolled up and stuffed between two couch cushions. She said, "Oh dear. Babies do knock us off our axis, don't they?" I guess that means everyone else is having a little bit of a hard time adjusting to Walter.

But not me!

He's supposed to wear one of the outfits one of The Ladies gave him at the baby shower. I think it's from Anne. Or maybe it's from Laure. I don't know which is which anyway. The outfit is a tiny blue suit, with a tie and everything.

When I carefully squeeze his little baby arms and legs into it, he looks even more like he works in a bank. He crinkles up his forehead and pushes his eyebrows together.

He looks like he's wondering why he has to wear an uncomfortable suit when he's not even a week old yet and we're not leaving the apartment. I wonder the exact same thing when Mom and Dad say to get dressed when we're not going anywhere.

Why can't I be in pajamas if we're just staying home? Why can't Walter? I shrug my shoulders. If it were up to me, The Ladies wouldn't be coming here at all. Vinegar. I do another shiver.

When they arrive, all of the dishes are washed, and the crumbs are swept up. The cushions are checked for wet diapers.

Grandma Balthazar answers the door and shows them inside to the living room. Mom is sitting next to me on the love seat. Walter is in his bouncer seat, looking concerned. He's a very smart baby.

"I'll go start a pot of coffee for everyone," says Grandma Balthazar. She walks back through the kitchen door, leaving Mom and Walter and me alone with Anne, Laure, and Lenae.

The Ladies are wearing pointy witch shoes again. They sit down on the couch across from us.

Only one of them is wearing a hat. It's not a witch hat. It's small and gray, and there is a tiny fake bird sitting on one side of it. The bird hat lady leans forward until her elbows are on her knees. I think her name is Laure. Or maybe it's

Lenae. She smiles at me with a hundred-tooth smile.

"I am glad you have been found, ma choupette. We were all so very worried when you ran from the bakery last week." She taps a finger on her chin. Her nail polish is the exact same color as her dress. It is the color of the inside of a banana. Not exactly yellow, but not exactly white.

"I'm sorry, dear. I cannot remember your name. Only that it is not—" she laughs into her banana-manicure hand "—Vinegar." The two other ladies laugh into their hands, too.

My face and neck feel like they are made of lava. My eyeballs get watery, and I swallow hard. Mom isn't laughing this time. Neither is Walter. He looks pretty mad, actually. His face looks almost as red as my face feels. He is shaking his little fists.

The lady with the bird hat notices Walter for the first time.

"Ah! And here is the baby! What a serious little baby." She looks at Mom. "May I hold him?"

Mom looks at me, and then she looks at Walter. He is still red and shaking. Mom smiles a big smile at the lady with the bird hat. "Of course! Be my guest!"

I don't want the lady to hold my baby brother, especially after she laughed about Vinegar all over again. But it kind of looks like Walter is about to—

"Oh là là! The baby has just—he smells like he—he must have dirtied his diaper! Please, my dress is very expensive. Someone take him before his diaper leaks!"

The lady holds Walter far away from her dress. Walter isn't red anymore, and he isn't shaking anymore. He looks pretty happy with himself.

Mom looks happy with Walter, too. "Oh dear," she says. "It smells like serious business. I'm going to have to excuse myself. This poor boy is going to need a bath and a change of clothes. You can wait in here if you'd like, but it might take awhile."

The three ladies look at each other. Mom looks at me and winks. I smile at her.

"Oui, of course," says the lady with the bird hat. "We do not want to keep you."

"We do not want to be in the way, either. It is so busy when there is a baby in the house!" says one of the other ladies. Anne or Laure or somebody. "We will see you back at the office, Alice." She wiggles her fingers at Mom like she's too tired to do an actual regular wave. "Enjoy your family time!"

Mom smiles. "I certainly will."

At the dinner table on Saturday night, Dad is laughing so hard he can't keep his broccoli on his fork.

"Did Walter really poop at that exact moment?" he asks.

Mom nods her head. "Just ask Winicker! She was right there for the whole thing!"

"I can't believe I missed it," says Grandma Balthazar. "Little Walter stuck up for his big sister. See, Winicker? Isn't it wonderful to have a sibling?"

I stop spreading butter on my roll for a second to look over at Walter. He's asleep in his bouncer. His tiny hands are on his belly, and when he breathes they go up and down. I nod at Grandma Balthazar. "Yeah, it actually is. I didn't think I would like it, but I do."

Mom and Dad and Grandma Balthazar get kind of quiet. At first I think it's because they're all chewing, but their forks are on their plates, and they're just smiling at each other and looking a little like they might cry at any second. I like when they're all happy at me, but I don't like when they happy cry. I cram the rest of my roll into my mouth and swallow and stand up fast.

"I'm going to go write a postcard to Roxanne. I haven't talked to her since right before the, um . . . the Eiffel Tower incident." *Incident* is the word Grandma Balthazar uses when something bad happened, but she doesn't want to bring the whole thing up all over again.

"Okay, honey," Mom says. "I'm going to get Walter settled into his bassinet, and then maybe the rest of us can watch a movie? When you're done writing to Roxanne, I mean."

Things aren't so bad here, even with a new baby. He does poop a lot, just like I thought he would, but his timing is great.

Roxanne,

I'm sorry I can't come visit after all. I'll visit someday, but not tomorrow or anything like that. I like my brother a lot, it turns out. Please give Lincoln a pat for me. And tell Granny Bee I said hi, and that I wish her recipe for chocolate de agua were not so top secret, because then Grandma Balthazar could make it for me here.

Love,

Winicker

PS

Actually, why don't you tell Granny Bee that I am still very sad about living in Paris and having a new baby brother. And then after that, tell her the recipe would probably make me feel a lot better.

Thanks.

GRANNY BEE'S

Top Secret Chocolate de Agua

INGREDIENTS

8 cups of water

4 cinnamon sticks

1 teaspoon cloves

1/4 teaspoon nutmeg

1/4 teaspoon salt

2 cups cocoa powder (unsweetened)

1 cup sugar

DIRECTIONS

Mix the water, cinnamon sticks, cloves, nutmeg, and salt. Bring to a boil over medium heat. Simmer until 1/3 of the liquid evaporates. Add cocoa and stir until it is well mixed. Add sugar to taste. Remove the cinnamon sticks and cloves. Serve hot.

Winicker Wallace's

¿Aló?: (Spanish) Hello?

Au revoir et bonne chance.: Goodbye and good luck.

Bienvenue: Welcome

Bon courage: Good luck

Bonjour: Good day

Boulangerie: Bakery

C'est magnifique: It's wonderful

Chocolate de Agua: (Spanish) A Dominican cinnamon-y hot chocolate drink

El bebé: (Spanish) The baby

Excusez-moi: Excuse me

Ho!: Oh!

J'ai besoin d'un médecin!: I need a doctor!

Je suis désolée: I'm sorry

La Tour Eiffel: The Eiffel Tower

Ma choupette: My little cabbage

Madame: Mrs.

Merci: Thank you

Métro: The subway system in Paris

Monsieur: Mr.

Oh là là: Oh dear

Oui: Yes

Pain au chocolat: Puffy pastry with chocolate inside

Parc Zoologique de Paris: The Paris zoo

Quel dommage: What a pity

Très chic: Very stylish

Meet the Author

Renee Beauregard Lute lives in the Pacific Northwest with one husband, two cats, and three amazing children. (Maddie, Simon, and Cecily, that's you!) There are many writers in the Pacific Northwest, and Renee is one of them. There may also be sasquatches in the Pacific Northwest, but Renee is not a sasquatch.

Like Winicker, Renee is from Western Massachusetts and loves macarons and sending postcards. Unlike Winicker, Renee has never lived in Paris, but she is very certain she would not hate it, even if Mirabel Plouffe lived next door.

Meet the Illustrator

Laura K. Horton is a freelance illustrator that has always had a passion for family, creativity, and imagination. She earned her BFA in illustration and animation from the Milwaukee Institute of Art and Design. When she's not working, she can be found drinking tea, reading, and game designing. Recently she has moved to Espoo, Finland, to obtain a master's degree in game design and development.